MOLLY LIKOVICH

Be Terrible: A Holiday Monster Romance

Third edition

ISBN: 9798778004627

Cover art by River Meade

This book was professionally typeset on Reedsy.
Find out more at *reedsy.com*

for all the girls who wished that Adam would have stayed a beast.

"I ask you to pass through life at my side—to be my second self, and best earthly companion."

-Jane Eyre

Contents

Playlist

- If I Can't Love Her by Terrence Mann
- Runaway by AURORA
- Homeland by Celtic Woman
- The Dawning of the Day by Celtic Woman
- Beauty & the Beast by David Bowie
- Heroes by David Bowis
- Within You by David Bowie
- For the Dancing and the Dreaming
- Heaven is Here by Florence + the Machine
- Cosmic Love by Florence + the Machine
- Mary on a Cross by Ghost
- Back From The Dead by Halestorm
- In The Woods Somewhere by Hozier
- Once Upon a Dream Lana Del Rey cover
- All is Found from Frozen 2
- Mine Forever by Lord Huron
- Not Dead Yet by Lord Huron
- Until the Night Turns by Lord Huron
- MIDDLE OF THE NIGHT By Loveless

- Restless Moon by Maya Hawke
- I Will Wait by Mumford & Sons
- Winter Winds by Mumford & Sons
- Snow & Ice by Sophia Anne Caruso
- willow by Taylor Swift
- The Great War by Taylor swift
- Run (Taylor's Version [From the Vault]) by Taylor Swift
- Pagan Poetry by Bjork
- A Thousand Years by Christina Perri
- Meet Me on the Equinox by Death Cab for Cuture
- Possibility by Lykke Li

LISTEN TO THE PLAYLIST <u>HERE</u>

Content Warnings

This book is intended for readers 18+ it contains darker themes that may be triggering to some readers. Please visit mollylikovich.com for a full list of triggers.

Part One: The Path of Pins and Needles

Krampusnacht

I grip the edge of the kitchen counter and wait for the anxiety attack to pass. The memories come flooding in of his hands knotted in my hair, dragging me out to the car. The sound of a door slamming shut and his roommates laughing on the other side.

I take a swig of wine and silently beg the anxiety meds to work faster. After a few moments I begin to feel the waves of panic recede and I'm able to breathe evenly again. I take my glass of wine and retreat out onto the back porch of Grandma Jo's beach house.

I sit down in a soft chair and look out at the ocean and stars, taking in the marvelous quiet that is the beach in the winter. No tourists or shouting children, just the sand and the sea.

I sip some more wine and look down at my hand holding the glass. I admire the ring on my right ring finger. It was Grandma Jo's. My sisters hadn't wanted it, saying it was too plain, but I love it. It's old and unique. Designed to look like it's made out of tree branches delicately woven together.

I twist it around once, twice, three times; my ADHD finding peace in the repetition. After a while, the meds, and wine, and the sound of the waves puts me right to sleep.

* * *

There is someone in the house. I sit up straight, startled awake from my dreamless sleep not by the sound of the waves but by the sound of heavy footsteps and chains rattling inside the house.

I stand up and step away from the sliding glass door, reaching into my back pocket for my phone, only to realize that I'd left it on the kitchen counter. And Grandma Jo's house is way out on the outskirts of town. There's no one around for miles. Nowhere to go. No one to call for help. I have two options: one, hideout in the sand all night and hope that whoever is inside doesn't find me, or two, sneak inside and try to get to my phone so I can call 911.

I choose option number two.

I tip-toe up to the sliding door and peek inside to see a large, looming shadow move across the front hall. If I'm fast enough about it I can run in and grab it before the intruder notices.

I slide the door open as softly as humanly possible and race barefoot across the dining room and into the kitchen. I see my phone sitting on the counter like a lighthouse guiding a ship in from a storm and I lunge for it. But in doing so I manage to knock over the half-drunk bottle of wine, sending it *and* my phone crashing to the floor. The bottle bursts into a cacophony of shattering glass and my phone slides across the tile and under the fridge.

I freeze. The shadow moves. The intruder has definitely heard me now and is headed my way. There's no way I can make it back to the sliding door without being seen so I guess it's time for surprise option number three.

Grandma Jo's gun.

The sound of the intruder's footsteps and *freaking chains* is getting closer. Even though I can feel another panic attack on the horizon, there's no time for wine and pill-popping now. I dash across the kitchen to the corner drawer and pull out the handgun. I check that it's loaded and hope that even though I've never shot a gun in my life I will somehow not fuck this up. I cradle the gun to my chest and crouch down behind the counter, waiting and praying.

"Erscheinen. Ich weiß, dass du da bist."

What the hell? Why is he speaking German?

I *am* fluent in German, it's my major after all, but I've yet to encounter any fluent German speakers here on the Eastern Shore of Maryland.

"Erscheinen. Erscheinen," the intruder says again.

Come out. Come out.

"Ich weiß, dass du da bist."

I know you're there.

The footsteps are so close, the chains rattling feels louder than thunder. I can't stand it. It's now or never. I click the safety and jump up, aiming the gun at the intruder.

"Stay back!" I shout. Then quickly remembering the intruder's German, I translate my words to, "Bleib zurück!"

The intruder laughs and rounds the hallway to stand before me in the kitchen.

"I speak English, little one."

My jaw drops in horror. I was expecting some sick, masochistic man to be stalking my halls. But there is no mistaking who this being before me is. Grandma Jo was a German immigrant, she raised me and my sisters on the stories of Germanic folklore.

"Krampus," I whisper in disbelief.

Then I fire the gun.

Turns out I have surprisingly good aim for never having shot a gun before. I hit Krampus in his shoulder and he roars. The sound reverberates off the walls, and I can practically feel my bones rattle beneath my skin. I drop the gun in shock and take a step back from the horrifying creature.

Krampus quickly regains his composure and faces me head-on.

"Well, little one, you were not my intended victim." He takes a step closer. "My intended victim, it would seem, isn't here." Another step. "I was going to leave." A final step.

Krampus stands right in front of me; looming over me. He's seven feet tall at least, and my puny five feet makes me feel minuscule before him. I tilt my head back, my body pressed up against the wall, my breath caught in my chest as I look into his red eyes.

Krampus reaches up to his shoulder where my bullet grazed him. He presses his fingers to the wound and they come away red with blood. I suck in a sharp and shallow breath at the sight. Krampus looks back at me. For a moment he pauses, studying me. I see a flash of uncertainty or...*disbelief* pass over his eyes. But then it's gone and replaced by a wicked grin.

"Well, now it seems I have a new victim."

Before I can protest, the ancient creature reaches out and wraps a clawed hand in my hair and pulls. I cry out in pain and surprise as he begins to drag me across the kitchen.

"Stop!" I shout. "Please!"

5

He just chuckles.

"Oh, it's too late for that, little one. You had your chance to be good."

He drags me down the front hall, one hand in my hair, the other gripping his chains. I kick and scream but I'm no match for this beast. When we reach the front door he throws me down to the floor next to a large velvet sack. He crouches over me and I look back up at him in fear.

"Since this is your first time coming along with me, I'll give you a choice." He reaches into his sack and produces a long rope. He holds the rope in one hand and the chains in the other. "Choose one."

I look back and forth between the two. I know this story. I know how it goes. I want to fight him and yet I know that is clearly impossible. I am not escaping this beast's clutches any time soon. So I decide to do what little I can to make this ordeal the least bit bearable for myself.

I gently tap the hand holding the rope. Krampus smiles.

"Good girl. Now give me your hands."

I remain silent as I hold my hands out in front of me. The beast wastes no time in binding my wrists together.

"Good," he says again. "Now your feet."

I shift back and let the beast bind my ankles together. Once he's finished he looks back into my eyes, his red ones full of wicked mischief.

"It's a long ride home," he says. "Are you going to scream? Do I need to gag you?"

"I—" I have no idea what to say. I look over at his sack and then back at him, realizing what he means. "No," I say softly. "I'll be quiet."

He reaches out and runs his fingers through my long, honey-blonde hair, his claws gently scraping my scalp. I shiver at his touch.

"Such a good girl. A shame you had to act so naughty."

I feel an entirely different anxiety than I did after Blair's phone call begin to wash over me. The initial shock of coming face to face with a thing of myth has begun to wear off and the true horror at the state of my situation is sinking in.

"Will you…" my voice trails off into a whisper. I find that I'm too scared to speak. The stories are about Krampus kidnapping children and punishing them for disobeying their parents. I have no idea what the protocol is for when a twenty-one-year-old college student accidentally shoots him in her kitchen. Grandma Jo seemed to have skipped that one.

"Will I do what?" Krampus asks.

"Be gentle?" I feel pathetic as the words leave my lips.

He chuckles and I feel another swell of anxiety rush through me. He strokes my hair once more and my anxiety begins to mix with *anticipation*? No. No, there is no way that I actually *like it* when Krampus touches my hair.

"If you're quiet, we will see. Now," he stands up straight again, and again I'm taken aback by his height. He leans down and scoops me into his arms with ease, "we must be off."

Then Krampus shoves me into his sack and throws it over his shoulder. I bite my lip, fighting the urge to scream in terror. If I scream he will gag me, and if he does that it means I'm not being quiet enough which means he won't be gentle and I do *not* want to know what that entails.

Krampus begins to walk on and I'm jostled back and forth against his back. I press my hands against my mouth and try to keep quiet as the beast carries me off to God knows where.

The cold winter night air starts to creep through the fabric of Krampus's sack causing me to shiver. I do my best to curl up but the constant jostling makes it virtually impossible. I eventually give up and try to make myself dead weight as my body is knocked around relentlessly as Krampus continues.

After what feels like a small eternity there is a sudden drop and I can no longer keep myself from screaming. I feel the weightless sensation of falling. Did he throw me off a cliff? Is this how punishments for adults work?

But before my mind can race any further into despair and doom, I feel the jolt of a landing and hear Krampus chuckle. Wherever I am, he is still with me. God, I hate how that suddenly makes her feel just the slightest tinge of comfort.

What is this? Stockholm Syndrome on overdrive?

Krampus keeps going, letting me get knocked around until I hear a door open and close, and then I'm dumped on the ground. I cry out again as I land hard on what feels like a stone floor.

Krampus opens the sack and grabs a fistful of my hair again. I grit my teeth and try to stay silent but I figure it's probably useless now that I've already made noise twice.

Krampus drags me completely out of the bag and settles me on my knees before him. He keeps his hand in my hair and pulls my head back so that my eyes meet his once more.

"I told you to be quiet, little one."

"Monika," I say softly, feeling like an idiot.

"Pardon?"

"Mein name ist Monika. Nicht klein."

The beast smirks. "So she knows German."

"I spoke German back at the house."

He tugs on my hair again, forcing me to keep my eyes on him.

"That you did. I am simply surprised that you know more than one phrase."

He pulls my hair a third time and I do my best not to hiss from the pain.

"Ich spreche fließend Deutsch," I say, somewhat proudly. If an ancient Germanic beast is going to torment me then I'm going to at least make it clear that I'm not some clueless American. I know my roots, and I know his language.

"Are you trying to impress me?"

"No," I say. "I just don't want to be called 'little one' all night."

At that, he laughs and I feel a chill run down my spine at the sound.

"What makes you think you're only staying the night?"

"I…"

"For a little German girl, you certainly don't know your legends very well." He leans down, one hand still in my hair, the other one cups my chin and I feel his claws dig in the tiniest bit. "When I take a victim, they stay with me until Christmas."

I open my mouth to speak but I don't know what to say. Should I beg? Should I fight? He's right, I apparently don't know this story very well.

"Now, meine Schöne, let's begin our fun, shall we?"

He yanks me up by my hair and I can't help but cry out again.

"See, meine Schöne, I told you to be quiet and I would be gentle. But you've made so much noise and now you must be punished."

He picks me up and throws me over his shoulder as he makes his way across the room which I now realize is a small cave. There's a large bed in one corner, a fireplace in the other, and before the fireplace, there are several chairs and a…

Bench.

I try to squirm against him, but his grip is ironclad, there's no escape. He sets me down on my feet and keeps one clawed hand on my two bound ones as he sits in the large red armchair before the fire.

"Now, meine Schöne, we'll start easy since you were quiet for *most* of the journey."

He tugs on my hands causing me to stumble forward. I try to catch my balance but he doesn't let me. He just chuckles again at my nervousness and pulls me down across his lap. Krampus smooths my hair down my back and once again knots his claws in it. He leans down close so that his mouth is right by my ear.

"Are you ready, meine Schöne?"

No I am not ready, but it seems pointless to fight him. Even if I said 'no can I have a minute' I highly doubt he would care.

"Yes," I whisper.

And then he hits me—*hard*.

I cry out from the impact of his hand hitting my ass. Before I even have time to process the stinging sensation, he does it again and again. I buck against him, crying out with each spank. After several blows Krampus stops and digs his nails into my ass, kneading my skin through the thick fabric of my jeans. I hear him groan softly and I'm really starting to think the stories about him are entirely wrong.

"You don't take children, do you?" I breathe.

Krampus stands me up again and I wobble on my bound feet but he holds me steady.

"No, meine Schöne. I don't."

He doesn't say anything else, just leans forward and undoes the rope around my ankles. I'm about to thank him but then his hands are at my waistband, undoing the buttons on my jeans.

"What are you doing?" I whisper.

"I think you know what I'm doing."

He pulls down the zipper and tugs my jeans down my legs.

I stumble once more and without thinking thrust my bound hands out to grip his shoulder to keep my balance. I feel him stiffen beneath my touch. I instinctively dig my fingers into the soft fur that covers his skin as he slides my pants the rest of the way down my legs.

He lets me keep holding onto him as I step out of my jeans and he tosses them aside. He stands me up straight again and just gazes at me; standing before him in nothing but my sweatshirt and little black underwear. The beast reaches out a hand for my lower regions but now that my feet are free I'm able to step back from him. He growls low in his throat when I do.

"Why?" I ask. "Why are you doing this?"

"Because you shot me."

"So now you're going to rape me?"

Krampus's mischievous face distorts into a look of confusion and...*hurt?*

"No," he says firmly, the growl still hardening his words. "Now come here."

I take another step away from him. "No," I say, letting the word sound strong on my tongue. "I shot you because you broke into my house."

"That was not your house. It is Josephine Brandt's house. What you were doing there is beyond me. But regardless, you committed an act of violence against me."

"And now you've committed one against me, so let me go."

He chuckles at that. I'm growing infuriated with how frequently he laughs at me.

"Do you think a few swats on your behind is the equivalent to a bullet?"

Admittedly, no. I feel like he has a point there.

"I'm not coming back over there on my own."

"Well, now that's just foolish. You know I can just drag you back. And while that's rather fun for me I'd imagine your scalp is growing sore by now. But," he stands up and I stumble back once more, "you're very beautiful and I do enjoy pulling your hair."

"Why were you in Josephine Brandt's house?"

"Why were you?" He asks as he steps nearer to me, closing out the space between us.

"Because she left it to me."

My words cause him to pause. For the first time since meeting him earlier that evening, he seems surprised.

"What do you mean by that?"

"Just that. She died and she left the house to me."

"Josephine is dead?" He says, his voice growing softer which I somehow find more unsettling than when he was growling.

"Yes," I say. "She died several years ago. I only go to the house during Christmas."

"Why would she leave it to you?" he demands.

"Because I'm her granddaughter."

Krampus looks down at me in confusion. I am really starting to wonder what the hell is going on.

"How do you know my grandmother?" I ask.

Krampus quickly regains his beastly demeanor and reaches out for my bound wrists.

"That is enough questions for now."

He leads me back over to his chair and spreads me across his lap once more. This time I don't fight him. I steel myself against him as he tangles his hand in my hair yet again and brings his other down my backside, harder than before. I scream again and again as he spanks me. He begins to move the hand in my hair down the back of my neck, his claws digging into my skin just enough to send chills throughout my body. He keeps spanking me without reprieve and I'm horrified to realize the arousing effect his violent ministrations are having on my body.

When Krampus finally stops hitting me I sigh softly and let my head loll against his knee. Even though he's shirtless, he's wearing tweed pants and the fabric feels soft and comforting against my flushed skin. Krampus begins to run his fingers through my hair as the hand that was spanking me goes to the waistband of my underwear. As one claw hooks around the fabric, I stiffen and try to move away. Krampus pushes my head back down, keeping me in place.

"Tell me, meine Schöne, if I were to strip these off right now and put my hand between your thighs, how wet would you be?"

"I'm not wet," I say, feeling both completely aroused and ashamed at the same time.

Who the hell started the rumor that this guy was a child thief? He's practically a freaking incubus.

Krampus chuckles yet again, softer this time, and slips his hand underneath the fabric of my underwear. I gasp at the cool sensation of the tip of his claw running down my sex.

"You're such a liar, meine Schöne," he says. "Do you know what happens to liars?"

He begins to drag his claw gently up and down my folds, slipping in between them to explore the wetness that's starting to pool between my thighs.

"They get punished," I whisper, fighting against all my common sense not to give in to how horribly wonderful this is beginning to feel.

"Correct."

He presses his finger deeper into my folds and I shudder from his touch. I can't help but imagine how good it would feel to have him thrust his fingers deep inside me, but then I remember his claws and I jerk away from his touch.

"Be still, meine Schöne," he says softly.

"It's going to hurt," I whisper.

"It won't," he says in a surprisingly gentle tone.

I want to argue with him but then I feel the sensation of his claws retract and nothing but the feel of his fingers remains on my sex.

What is he, a cat? Retractable claws for sexual purposes only.

I hold my breath as the beast slides one finger inside me.

"Relax, meine Schöne," he murmurs.

I try to exhale slowly as he inserts his finger into me and curls it against my inner wall, hitting my g-spot perfectly. I gasp from the sensation as he runs his other hand back up to grasp the back of my neck. He begins to pump his finger against me and soon adds a second. His inhumanely large hand has just two fingers filling me up more than I was ready for. He begins to move faster and I can't help but moan from the forbidden pleasure of his touch.

"Good girl," he whispers, scraping his claws along my spine, causing another shiver to rack my body.

He moves his fingers in and out harder and harder until I'm on the brink of an unholy climax when he suddenly stops, withdrawing his hand. I let out a pathetic whimper at the sudden emptiness I feel without the pressure of his fingers inside me. He chuckles again in that irritating way.

"That was your punishment for lying, meine Schöne," he says as he smooths my hair away from my face.

I want to slap him.

But he'd probably like that.

He suddenly stands, bringing me up with him, my wrists *still* bound. He looks down at me, the wicked look in his eyes is gone and replaced with one that seems almost jovial. Like he enjoys my presence. Maybe he does if only for the sick pleasure he gets from tormenting me.

And maybe I'm getting some sick pleasure from it as well.

"It is time to rest, meine Schöne."

I hold out my bound wrists and he eyes them idly.

"You expect me to sleep tied up?"

He laughs and shakes his head then undoes the bounds. There are red marks on my wrists from where the ropes have dug into my skin, I rub them, trying to alleviate some of the pain.

Krampus watches me intently. He takes one of my hands in his. "Come," is all he says as he leads me deeper into his cave. I follow him, my bare feet padding across the cool stone floor until we reach a small pool in a darkened corner of the cave, almost completely hidden in shadows. The only light comes from some candles burning in the corner; the scent of peppermint and pine trees wafting through the air. He brings me closer to the pool and I realize there's steam coming off the water. He gestures for me to get in. I look down at my sweatshirt and underwear, debating if I want to get my only clothes wet or get naked in front of this...*man.*

"Get in the water, meine Schöne."

"Turn around," I say softly.

He smirks.

"Why would I do that?"

"Because I don't want you to look at me."

"But you see," he runs his hand up my arm to cup the back of my neck, "I *do.*"

I try to shift away from him but he keeps a firm grip on me.

"You can undress or I'll do it for you."

15

"Is this a punishment?" I whisper.

He strokes his thumb up and down my spine, the tip of his claw gently raking through the hair at the nape of my neck.

"No," he says simply. "I am trying to help you."

"I can do it myself."

He tilts his head and smiles knowingly. "Take off your clothes."

I take a step back and reach down and grab the hem of my sweatshirt and pull it up and over my head so that I'm now clad in nothing but my bra and underwear. His eyes move across my body, blatantly taking in the sight of my nearly naked figure. He steps closer to me.

"Take off the rest," he says softly.

I tilt my head to look up at him. "Who are you?" I whisper.

"You know the answer to that."

"This is nothing like the stories."

"Maybe the stories are lies created by fearful men."

He rests his hand on my shoulder and begins to drag it across my collarbone, his claws scratching the surface of my skin, enough to cause me to gasp softly, but not deep enough to pierce the skin.

"What did these men have to fear?" I ask softly, keeping my eyes on his. Their once fiery red glow has now faded to a softer amber. There is a wanting look to them that is not as vicious as the one he gave me when we met only a few hours ago.

"Monsters," he says as he slides his fingers under one of my bra straps.

"Like you?"

"Like what they decided I am."

"Which brings me back to, who are you?"

He pushes some of my hair behind my shoulder. "Be quiet

now, meine Schöne."

He pushes the straps of my bra down and then gently turns me around so that my back is to him. I inhale sharply as he unhooks my bra and lets it fall away. I instinctively go to cover my breasts but the beast reaches out for my arms and pulls them away.

"Be still," he commands.

I don't know why, but I nod. I feel ridiculous, having gone from fighting him to obeying him with ease over the course of one night.

He drags a claw down my spine and I shiver. He brings it lower and lower until he reaches my underwear again. He hooks a finger inside and begins to slide them down my legs. I step out of them and then I am completely naked before an ancient beast of Germanic folklore.

This really isn't how I saw my holidays going.

"Turn around now."

I shake my head.

"Turn around, meine Schöne, or I'll have to punish you again."

Thinking about his brutal ministrations to my disobedience is more than enough to persuade me. I turn slowly back around to face him and let him take in the sight of my naked body.

He puts his hands on me and drags them down my sides, coming to rest on my ass. He grips my flesh hard and pulls me toward him with a grunt. I gasp again as I stumble closer, my hands going out to land on his chest.

"You take women," I whisper, not a question. A statement.

"I took one," is his only response. "No more questions, meine Schöne."

He then sinks to his knees before me, his horned head level with my stomach.

17

"What are you doing?"

"Rewarding you for your obedience."

"You don't…have to."

He looks up at me and smirks, enough that I can see his fangs glinting in the candlelight.

"I don't *have* to do anything, meine Schöne."

"But—"

"Be quiet," he says, his voice a little more forceful.

And then he leans forward and presses his mouth to my sex. I gasp and lean forward from the intense sensation of his tongue against me. My hands go to his large horns and hold on to keep my balance as he slips his long tongue (oh my god, *how* is it this long?) inside me. He curls it against my inner walls and I whimper from the delicious pleasure this beast is inflicting upon me.

I want to say his name as he pleasures me relentlessly but he never actually told me it's Krampus, and even as he's here, kneeling before me with his tongue between my thighs, it feels absurd to address him as a thing from fairytales.

So I let my moaning suffice as he flicks his tongue across my clit. I grip his horns harder and cry out. I am so close and I'm terrified that he'll deny me my orgasm again as punishment. I'm terrified this is a trick. It's bad enough that I'm apparently attracted to a demonic mythical being who dragged me here in a bag, but what's worse would be for said demonic being to then not even let me get off.

My fears are all dashed away when he nips at my clit at the same time that his uncannily long tongue slides inside me again and pushes in and out, unabated. I practically scream as he grips the back of my thighs and tongue-fucks me to completion.

"Now," he says, pulling away from me, his hands still gripping the backs of my thighs, "get in the pool."

Sehr gut

I nod, feeling numb and dazed from my orgasm, and walk over to the edge of the pool. I sit down and slowly slide into the steamy water. It feels marvelous against my chilled bones and raw, red wrists. I sigh softly and sink deeper. I close my eyes and lean my head back but open them again when I hear the sound of Krampus getting in the water with me.

"What are you—"

He reaches out and grabs me by the arm and drags me over to him. I yelp in surprise as the beast brings me to straddle his lap.

"Let me go," I say.

He laughs in amusement. "I think I've already established that I'm not going to. Not anytime soon at least. You're much too fun."

"I—" he laughs again at my shocked expression. "Does that mean you're not going to punish me anymore?"

Another laugh.

"Don't be ridiculous, meine Schöne. This is just a brief

reprieve for some good behavior." He leans forward and drags his tongue up the length of my neck causing me to gasp loudly and dig my hands into his fur. He circles my ear with his tongue and nips at the lobe. "Your ordeal with me has only just begun."

"Why?" I breathe, as he continues to lick and bite my ear and the soft skin of my neck around it.

"Because you shot me."

"I thought you were trying to kill me."

He digs his claws into my hair and turns my head to the side so that he can begin his oral assault on the other side of my neck. I dig my fingers deeper into his surprisingly soft fur as he licks the column of my throat once more.

"I had done nothing to you," he purrs in my ear.

"You broke into my house."

"It was Josephine Brandt's house, you just happened to be there."

"I told you she's dead," I say breathlessly as he sticks his long tongue in my ear and moves it in methodical circles. "It's my house now. And you broke in."

"There was no need for violence," he says, tauntingly.

He tugs on my hair, bringing my head back so that the whole of my throat is exposed to him. He licks down further until he reaches where my neck meets my shoulder and he digs his fangs in deep. I scream and grip him harder as he laughs around the newly inflicted wound.

"Let me go," I whimper as he licks the bite mark. "Please."

"No," he murmurs as he licks me lower and lower.

I try to shift away but he's far too strong and he simply lifts me higher out of the water so that he can take my breast in his mouth. He flicks his tongue against my already hardened nipple and then bites me there as well and I scream again.

21

"Stop," I pant.

"Why?" He asks, sounding genuinely curious.

"It hurts."

"Yes, meine Schöne, it's supposed to."

He takes my nipples between his fingers and gently pricks them with his claws as he pulls on them. I whimper and let myself fall forward, my head landing against his shoulder. He chuckles once more and nuzzles his face into my hair but refuses to let go of my nipples no matter how much I squirm.

"I can tell you enjoy this, meine Schöne."

He's right. I do. This is so wrong. He terrifies me and excites me all at once. Every time he touches me I'm overcome with a completely foreign sense of euphoria. I have never had any lovers besides Blair, and his caresses had quickly turned to violence. And where Blair's violence came from hatred, Krampus's seems to come from pleasure. He can tell I enjoy the pain as much as he enjoys inflicting it.

"Tell me the truth," he whispers in my ear. "Do you like when I touch you?"

He rolls my already sensitive nipples in his fingers then pulls again and I moan.

"Yes," I whisper, resting my head in the crook of his neck.

He releases my breasts and slides one hand down into the water where he roughly cups my sex, his claws gently grazing me. I grab onto him again and gasp.

"Do you like when I hurt you, meine Schöne?"

"Yes," I rasp.

I can feel him smile as he kisses the side of my neck. His lips are so soft and their sweet press is so gentle that it riots against all the previous violent affections he's shown towards me.

"Good girl. Come."

In one fluid motion, he picks me up and rises from the pool. I inhale sharply as the cool winter air hits my skin.

"You'll be warm soon," he says as he carries me back out to the main part of his cave.

I quickly realize what he means as I see him pass the armchair and head for the bench. It's red like the armchair and clearly not designed for sitting.

He sets me down and walks to the other side of the bench where there sits another velvet sack. He pulls something out and I hear the tell-tale rattle of chains.

"What are you doing?" I ask, taking a step away from the bench.

He looks back at me. "Don't walk away from me."

He walks over to me and takes my hand and drags me over to the bench. He pushes me down on my stomach, spreading me across it. I feel the air get knocked out of me as my stomach presses down against the plush satin cushioning on top. He holds both my hands firmly and clamps two shackles to them.

"What? Kra—" I stop myself from saying his name, but he catches it on my tongue.

He releases my hands, now shackled to a chain connected to the cave wall, and crouches down so that he's at eye level with me.

"Do you want to call me something, meine Schöne?"

"Yes," I whisper.

"Very well," he says, standing back up. He runs his fingers through my hair, gently this time. "You may call me mein Herr." He releases my hair and picks up another chain, this one has—to my horror—a collar on the end.

"I'm not a pet," I say, trying to sound as firm as possible when really I'm shaking from the cold, and fear, and horribly wanton anticipation.

He takes my face in his hand and traces a claw gently down the curve of my jaw.

"Of course you're not. But you *are* mine."

"I don't know you," I whisper.

He strokes my face again. "Be my good girl and I will show you."

He runs his thumb across my mouth and I part my lips without thinking so that he can slip it inside. While most of his body is covered in soft fur, his hands—like his face—are smooth skin that feels as soft as the cushioning beneath me.

"Can you do that, meine Schöne? Take this punishment and I'll tell you who I am."

With his other hand, he places it on one of my shackled ones, his fingers twirling Grandma Jo's ring.

"Okay, mein Herr."

He smiles. "Good."

He picks the collared chain back up and gently clasps it around my neck. But instead of attaching the chain to the wall as he did with my shackles, he leaves it hanging loose to the ground as he moves around behind me and I hear him pick something up. I wait in horrible suspense as his heavy footsteps make their way back to me.

He reaches down and picks the chain up off the ground and pulls. I inhale sharply in surprise as he pulls, bringing my head back towards him, exhibiting total control over me and my body.

"Are you ready for your third punishment, meine Schöne?"

"Yes, mein Herr."

He chuckles softly, but this time it sounds playful, not cruel like it did before. He gives the chain another tug and I feel the slightest pressure applied to my throat from the collar. Not enough to choke me, but enough to make me gasp. Then I feel something hit my backside. I immediately cry out in pain and arousal. I try to look over my shoulder to see what he's using to punish me and I see that it's the birch.

I guess the stories got that part right.

He hits me again, and again I cry out. I try to shift forward on instinct. It feels so good but it hurts so badly and the euphoric pain is muddling my mind. I have no idea if I want to escape it or endure it.

He swats me again and again with the birch and each time the stinging sensation intensifies. I can feel the wetness slick between my thighs as he continues the brutal punishment.

Soon my cries turn to screams and I realize I'm going to come from him spanking me alone.

"Good job, meine Schöne, scream for me."

He keeps beating my ass and I keep screaming until I reach my peak. I feel my orgasm rack my entire body, shattering me to pieces. But he gives me no reprieve, he just keeps hitting me.

"Mein Herr," I pant as the beautiful abuse continues.

"We're not done yet, meine Schöne."

"I've been punished," I whine. I've already orgasmed twice in one night. With Blair, I rarely came at all. I don't know how my body could possibly take a third climax, and if he keeps spanking me with that wicked tool then I am most certainly going to.

He stops whipping me and lets go of the chain. One of his claws drags down my back again and this time I can feel him draw blood.

"Mein Herr," I breathe.

I feel his lips kiss their way down my spine, licking up the

25

blood created by his claws and then he undoes the clasp of the collar and it falls away to the cave floor. He walks back around in front of me and undoes my shackles. I try to stand up but he pushes me back down.

"We're not done here, meine Schöne," he says as he yet again twists his fingers in my hair.

"I've been punished," I say, hating how pathetic I sound.

"It is not for you to decide when we're done."

He quickly flips me over so that I'm laying on my back. He comes to stand beside me, sliding the hand that was in my hair to come and rest around my throat, taking the place of the collar.

"You've screamed so beautifully for me tonight, but I haven't gotten the chance to see your face when you do."

I don't know what to say. I open my mouth to respond, but he silences me by slipping his thumb between my lips again and pressing on my tongue, silently commanding me to suck. I do. He lets his other hands trail down my stomach slowly, his claws pricking my sensitive skin.

"Are you going to scream for me, meine Schöne?"

He removes his thumb from my mouth but I only nod in answer. To that he squeezes my throat, lightly choking me. I move one of my hands to grab ahold of his wrist, he smiles down at me, that wicked look of mischief returns to his eyes.

"Answer me, meine Schöne. Will you scream for me?"

"Yes, mein Herr."

"Good girl." He brings his hand back up from my stomach to rest against my collarbone. "Do not hold back. If you do, I will only continue to punish you."

"Mein Herr," I pant against his chokehold on me.

"I will spank your beautiful bottom for hours until I get to see your face when I bring you to orgasm and hear you scream for me. Is that understood?"

"Yes, mein Herr."

"Good girl."

Then he digs his claws into my chest, drawing blood, and I cry out. Not a full scream, not yet. His punishments are quickly building up my pain tolerance, so even as he drags his claws down between my breasts and all the way to my stomach, drawing thin red lines the entire way, I am not yet at my peak of pain.

"Hmm," he says, studying the thin scratches he's left across my flesh. "You're not loud enough."

He moves his hand to my blonde curls above my sex and pulls on them like he did the hair on my head. I gasp and buck my hips up against his hand without thinking.

"Ah," he says, beginning to slide his fingers lower, "Is this how I make you scream, meine Schöne?"

I don't answer, I'm too breathless, his other hand still on my throat.

In response to my silence, he retracts his claws and thrusts three fingers inside me, causing me to cry out louder.

"Next time you ignore my question I'm chaining you back up. Is this how I get you to scream?"

"Yes, mein Herr," I pant.

"Good girl."

And then he finger fucks me harder than I've ever been in my life. He removes the hand from my throat to use those fingers to stimulate my clit while his other hand pumps in and out of me. I tilt my head back, close my eyes and moan so loud I think the stars in the sky can hear me.

"Are you going to come, meine Schöne?"

"Yes, mein Herr," I breathe.

"You may not come until you're screaming. You must beg me to come."

"Please let me come," I pant.

"Not until you scream."

I inhale sharply, trying to make sense of my thoughts but they're all coming too quickly, and then he pulls back and slaps my pussy—hard. I finally scream, bucking and panting like a wild animal from this sinful, magnificent pleasure this wicked beast has caused me.

As I ride my aftershocks down, Krampus folds himself over my body on the bench and presses a gentle kiss to my forehead. I am so taken aback by this gentle gesture, and so desperate to feel safe that I wrap my arms around his neck and pull him down closer to me.

Once I realize what I've done, I expect him to push me away or punish me again for trying to take control. But instead, to my immense surprise, he wraps his arms around me too, scooping behind my back and lifting me off the table. He sets me down on my feet and rests his forehead against mine, leaning down to close out the great difference in our heights.

I finally open my eyes again and look into his, their soft amber glow having returned in the aftermath of the ordeal. I start to slide my arms away from where I'm holding on to him, but he takes hold of my hands as I pull them away and place them against his chest. I can feel his heart beating almost as fast as mine.

"Do you still wish to know who I am, meine Schöne?"

I nod. "Yes," I whisper. "Tell me. Why does all this feel…"

"Natural?" He asks.

I nod again.

He leans down and rests his forehead against mine. This is all so strange. This night has been a whirlwind wilder than the snowstorm outside.

He twists the ring on my finger once more. I watch as he spins it around and around methodically. He seems enraptured by it.

"It has been so long since I've seen this ring," he says softly.

"What?" I ask.

"Josephine Brandt stole it from me centuries ago."

Kingeln

"Are you telling me my grandmother was centuries old?"

"Come, meine Schöne," he says as he takes my hand and leads me over to the large bed in the far corner of the room. He pulls back the red blanket and gestures for me to lay down.

I should probably protest one more time that he should let me go, but I know that's not going to happen, and even if it did, what would I be going back to? A lonely Christmas alone? Blair gone, having left behind nothing but bruises inside and out. A family that was too self-absorbed to notice how much pain I was in. An empty beach house full of haunted memories. How sad must I be to find more comfort here with a beastly being from my bedtime stories?

I climb under the covers and despite the brutal winter winds outside that move through the cave walls, the satin blanket warms my skin and feels like heaven to touch. Krampus, still fully nude from having bathed with me, gets in the bed on the other side.

He reaches out and takes my right hand, fingering the ring once more.

"Josephine Brandt has existed for a long time. That's why I was so surprised to hear you say that she passed."

"Grandma Jo was nearly a hundred years old," I say. "She was old but not centuries old. You're…" he looks at me expectantly, practically daring me to say it. And unlike when the night began, I feel bolder now. Perhaps when a beast touches you, you come out a bit more beastly yourself. "You're Krampus. You're a thing of myth."

"And yet here I am before you."

I reach out and tentatively place my hand against his cheek. I see another flicker of surprise in his eyes.

"You feel real."

He places a hand on top of mine. "I am, meine Schöne."

"Why do you call me that?"

He weaves his long fingers with mine and moves my hand down to his chest again to rest over his heart.

"You did not want to be called 'little one.'"

"But meine Schöne? That means *my lovely* in German."

He laughs softly. "I *am* German. And, clearly, so are you."

"Grandma Jo was an immigrant," I say, moving my thumb across the back of his hand.

"She was, but from a much longer time ago than she let you ever know. Long ago, when she was your age, she lived in a village near here."

"Where is *here?*" I ask. "You walked us here from the outskirts of Ocean City Maryland. I was never great at geography in elementary school, but I know that's nowhere near Germany."

He chuckles again in amusement and for the first time all night, the sound makes me smile.

31

"It is not. We are not in Germany, meine Schöne, we're in between the worlds. Josephine's childhood home lay near the border between your world and the one beyond. My world."

"But does that mean Ocean City is near too?"

"No," he says. He taps my ring with one finger. "The border between this world and mine shifts and changes as the years pass. I crossed over time and time again searching for this ring." He looks into my eyes again. "Searching for you."

He twists the ring once again. I look down at it again, realizing just what the woven pattern looks like it's made of.

Birch.

"Why did she steal it? Why is it so important? *How* did my grandmother live to be impossibly old?"

He smiles once more. "You're so talkative now."

He reaches his other hand behind me and pinches my behind. It's still sore from his many beatings and I yelp softly from the small pain. He chuckles and wraps his arm around me to pull me closer.

"You took your punishments like the good girl you are so I will answer all your questions. Josephine lived so long the way I do—magic. She was a powerful sorceress and a jealous one too. She stole this ring to punish me for loving a human. She, like many that came before her and long after, did not think a creature like me was deserving of love. After several centuries of being feared and hated it became easy to give into it. But I never punished children, that was just a cruel rumor that began so many years ago. I have been here since long before those silly stories were ever first told, and I will be here long after they cease to pass people's lips."

"But," I say softly, trying to process all his impossible words, "why was the ring so important?"

He reaches up and cups his hand behind my neck like he's done so many times this evening, and each time he does it, it feels more and more comforting.

"Monika," he says softly.

I inhale sharp and soft. It's the first time he's said my name since we encountered each other back at the beach house, what feels like an eternity ago even though it's only been hours.

"Because it was yours."

Wölfin

One of my favorite fairy tales was always Little Red Riding Hood. But not Grimm or Perrault, the darker, grittier versions. The ones that were passed by word of mouth between women in villages as opposed to the ones rich white men stole and then committed to paper for money.

The Tale of Grandmother told the story but with a sensual werewolf seducing an older, more mature Red Riding Hood into bed. She strips for him, she crawls into his embrace, and then upon realizing his true beastly nature she flees from him. He tries to catch her but is unsuccessful.

When I went to college I knew I wanted to keep studying fairy tales. I read Angela Carter's *The Bloody Chamber* and reveled in the grotesque, dark beauty of the stories, particularly *The Company of Wolves*. And Germanic folklore was rife with dark tales. Once I was able to peel away the thin and hollow layer that was the nonsense, watered-down version the Grimm Brothers created, I was able to get to the darkness lurking beneath.

Blair was the one to convince me to change my concentration

in my major from the history of the German language to Germanic Folklore. I met him my sophomore year when I got locked out of my dorm. He was the best friend of my RA, Rob. He sat in the hall with me and waited for Rob to get back. For the first time in ages I felt like I'd found someone who liked to hear me speak about my passions, and not only that, *believed* in them.

It only took a few more encounters for me to fall in love with him.

By the end of the year, he asked me to be his girlfriend and I said yes. I went home with him and crawled into his bed like Red Riding Hood did the wolf's, but unlike Red, I wasn't smart enough to realize my mistake in time to escape.

He loved me and I was so lonely it ached. Little girls dream of becoming princesses and living inside fairy tales because all they know is what Disney and Grimm have told them. Simple stories with sweet morals. But I knew that true fairy tales are the stuff of nightmares, and life with Blair was surely that.

Come Junior year I moved in with him and then the bruises became external to match the endless purple patches his verbal and sexual assaults inflicted upon my heart.

"I wish you'd just hit me," I said once during a fight. "Then at least everyone would know I wasn't crazy!"

I let another year pass in that nightmarish fairy tale. I crawled into his bed because sometimes I thought I could find true love and compassion there. He was loving more often than he hurt so I became a foolish maiden; a walking cliche.

Until Thanksgiving of my senior year.

This past Thanksgiving.

I walked from our apartment to the campus counseling center in the rain because I 'wasn't allowed to use his car. When I came stumbling in the door, soaking wet and sobbing, the girl at the front desk asked me what was wrong.

"I think my boyfriend rapes me."

Since then I couldn't even sit near another man without my skin crawling. A first-date kiss with another guy in my major led to a full-blown PTSD episode. And my family didn't 'believe' in therapy. I had to get the meds from my primary care. That and wine had to suffice for any kind of treatment.

It was a terrible love affair that ended in horrific heartbreak and a broken spirit. I did not think it was something I would ever overcome. Twenty years old and already ruined.

So what is happening here tonight in this cave between the worlds? How did simple kisses trigger me but being chained up and spanked didn't? How did I go from fear to comfort so quickly? I like to think I'm too smart to fall for fairy tale tricks twice in a matter of a few years.

"How was it mine?" I ask as I watch him spin Grandma Jo's ring around my finger.

"Because I knew you before. Before you lived this life inside these bones. Before your name was Monika. Before something happened to put such sadness in your eyes."

My breath stills in my throat for a moment. His amber eyes burning into mine. Why does it feel like I know him? Is what he's saying really true? It's impossible but if tonight has proved anything it's that the impossible is certainly doable.

"Are you telling me reincarnation is real?"

"I've lived a long life, meine Schöne. I have seen souls leave this world only to come back centuries later with no memory of the life they lived in the past. I hoped without hope that we would meet again. And now here you are. What is it true believers say? A Christmas Miracle? That's what you being here right now is."

I can't help but smile at that.

"Did I look the same back then?" I ask. "How did you know it was me?"

"You look the same," he murmurs, running his fingers through my hair. "But I knew for sure it was you when I saw the ring."

"If you knew it was me then why did you…"

He smirks. "Tie you up and drag you here?"

I shove him playfully. "Yes, that."

He leans in closer to me, our foreheads pressed together, our lips almost touching.

"I wanted to have some fun, and back when I knew you in your other life you liked things rough, so I took a guess that you'd feel the same now."

"What if I hadn't?"

"Then I would've stopped. But you said it yourself, you like it when I hurt you."

I gently trace my thumb across the back of his knuckles.

"I do," I say softly. "But I like this too."

He smiles. "As do I, meine Schöne."

And then he kisses me.

How strange that we've been so physical this evening, that he's touched me in ways no one ever has before, but we had not yet kissed. And now this kiss feels more passionate and intimate than anything else we've done.

I wrap my arms around his neck and he drags me on top of him. He rakes his claws down my back, creating more red marks across my skin, marking me as his.

The more time I spend with him the more my heart remembers what my mind can't.

I knew him once, back before he was a monster in my fairy

tales he was a man I wanted. He was somehow a man I loved.

This vicious beast was mine once upon a time.

"Let me make love to you, Monika," he murmurs against my mouth.

"You don't want to punish me anymore?" I say.

He chuckles. "Make no mistake, meine Schöne, I enjoy tormenting you as much as you enjoy taking my punishments, but right now I want to be inside you. Let me show you how I once loved you. Let me show you that I can do it again."

"Okay," I breathe.

He reaches down and lifts my hips up so that he can position himself between my legs and then he slams me down on his cock and I gasp from the intense pressure. If I thought his fingers filled me up, they were nothing compared to this.

"You're so big," I breathe as I let my head fall forward and burrow in the fur of his neck.

He digs his claws into my ass, causing me to moan.

"You can take it, meine Schöne."

I whimper in response as he slowly begins to thrust up into me.

"Look at me, Monika," he commands.

He yanks on my hair again and I manage to pull myself up again so that I'm sitting up straight, my hands braced on his chest.

"Move with me," he says.

I do as he says. I rock back and forth as he thrusts deeper and deeper into me and soon I'm crying out and he's groaning and it feels as if we're the only two people in the world.

Whichever men abused me before no longer matter. Whatever traumas I suffered begin to fade away. This night has washed the slate clean. The bruises on my heart are finally beginning to heal.

"Monika," he rasps as we continue to move together, building towards a crescendo.

He sits up and wraps his arms around my back and presses his mouth to mine as he thrusts one final time and I moan against his mouth as my orgasm washes over me. And at this moment memories wash over me.

Memories of another girl in another life.

Part Two: Stray from the Path

Long Ago...

***

"Don't wander off," Mother calls to me as I head out into the snow.

"You know I never do," I call back to her.

She heads into our house as I pull my hood up over my head to protect from the wind and falling snow, and head off into the woods.

It doesn't take me long to find the veil. The place where our world meets the edge of his. Not everyone can see it because not everyone is looking, but I've been looking for him all my life. My Seelenfreund. *Soulmate.* I used to think such things were just the stuff of stories, not something any living soul could be lucky enough to have.

Oh, how wrong I was.

I cross the threshold between the world and emerge into the forever winter of his world. This small place is nestled between the living and the dead. He is sitting in a chair by the fire, reading a book I left with him last time I visited.

It's my book. A story I came up with and left for him to find, hoping he would be moved by my words.

He looks up when he sees me enter. He smiles, places the book down, and comes to take me in his arms. He presses his lips to mine and the whole world makes sense again.

"Meine Schöne," he says, "I've missed you."

"And I, you. I came as soon as I could, but the men in the village…"

He frowns. "Are looking for a beast. Yes, I know."

"I know you're not responsible for the deaths. children suffer at the mercy of wolves and bears in the woods." I say gently, placing my hand over his heart. "You are not the monster they fear you are."

"Make no mistake, Rose," he says, taking a step back, "I am a monster, but not the kind they think."

He means he is not a child thief. He does not slip in during Yule to rip children from their beds and punish them brutally for sins all children tend to be guilty of committing.

"How are you monstrous, meine Liebe?"

He shakes his head as he sits back down in his chair.

"You always call me that."

"My love?" I say. "Because you are."

I walk over to him and take his face in my hands. "Do you think we met by mere chance that spring day in the meadow? You were meant to be mine as I was meant to be yours."

He places one of his large, clawed hands over my small one.

"You can never truly be mine," he whispers. "The world out there will never welcome a beast like me."

"Then I'll come to this world."

He looks into my eyes, his sorrow slowly turning to disbelief.

"Rose," he whispers.

"I mean it."

I reach to the side of the chair and pick up the small book I'd left with him. The story of Rose Red and The Beast. A girl in a red cape who finds true love and passion with a creature in the woods instead of the oppressive ideals of her small town full of small-minded people. I take his hands and place the book in them.

"Let me love you," I whisper.

"I am terrible, Rose," he says. "I have killed, I have killed your kind. I have done terrible things to you."

"No, you haven't."

"The people in your town would see what we do here as terrible."

"Then be terrible," I say fiercely. "And love me in all your wicked ways. I don't care how you love me, just as long as you do."

I take his hands in mine again and place them on my hips.

"Do you hear me, Krampus?" I whisper, stepping closer to him. "Love me. Be wicked. Be terrible. Just love me."

He stands up and takes me in his arms, pressing his mouth to mine. And then he's dragging me across the cave and over to the far wall on the other side of the fireplace. He takes the chains hanging from the wall and clasps the shackles around my wrists. I smile against his lips as he chains me to the wall, putting me at his mercy just as he knows I adore when he does. I feel completely free and unburdened when I put myself in his hands.

He picks up a riding crop from the other side of the room and stalks back to me. He digs his claws into my hair and pulls my head back.

"Should I punish you, meine Schöne?" he murmurs.

"Yes, mein Herr," I say.

43

He grins and then rips off my dress. Once I'm bare before him he cups my sex in his hand, lightly digging his claws into my flesh.

"Are you ready?" he asks, leaning in close and whispering in my ear. "I'm going to beat your body until it's as rose-red. I'm going to remind you that you're mine. Always. You don't belong to any of the men in that village, you belong to me and only me."

"Only you," I whisper happily.

And then he hits my pussy with the riding crop. I tilt my head back against the wall and cry out as he strikes me again and again. The pain is bliss.

After he's done slapping my sex he spins me around roughly, keeping a hand on the back of my neck to hold me in place as he uses the crop between my thighs, reddening the sensitive skin there. I moan and scream and bask in the horrible pleasure he's inflicting.

He drops the crop and brings his hand down across my ass, sending a beautiful shock of pain throughout my whole body. He does it again and again. I'm a sweaty, panting mess by the time he finishes with me. He spins me back around and takes my breasts in his hands, pinching my nipples roughly, digging in his claws, causing me to hiss from the pain.

"Do you think these are red enough, meine Schöne?"

I shake my head. "No, mein Herr. I don't think they are."

He leans down and takes one of my nipples in his mouth and bites down until I scream and my blood is trickling onto his tongue. He does the same to the other and then picks the crop up again and uses it on my breasts.

Once my body is red all over from his ministrations he unchains me and carries me to the bed. He throws me down and climbs on top of me with animalistic desire. I spread my legs and let him in. We move together in a wild state of lust. And I scream for him over and over again.

"Good Lord above, what devilry is this?"

We pull apart to see Josephine Brandt standing at the foot of the bed, with several of the village men in tow.

They followed me.

I had thought Josephine was my friend. I had confided in her that I had a new lover who didn't live in town, but I never expected this. I never for a second thought that she would've been able to figure out that I was in love with Krampus, the Yule Devil.

"Josephine," I say, sitting up and reaching towards my ripped dress on the floor.

"It's alright, Rose," Thomas, one of the village men, says. "We're here to save you."

"I don't need saving," I say. "Now go, get out of our home."

Josephine and the other men stare at me, mouths agape.

What happened next is a blur. The men race forward and drag me away from Krampus. He looks into my eyes and for the first time in all these nights I've known him, he looks afraid.

They rush towards him and I scream like a wild animal as I try to fight my way to him, but their hands are too strong. Some of the men drag me outside as others remained behind to try and fight him. As I'm dragged across the snow I hear him roar in rage as Josephine comes rushing out of the cave after me as I kick and scream. The men and Josephine drag me further across the border between the worlds and then leave me in a naked, weeping heap deep in the woods, covered by the fast falling snow.

Josephine leans down over me, a wicked smile on her face. I

look up at her through tear-stained eyes. I have never felt more hate in my heart than I do right now.

"What is wrong with you?" I say.

She takes my face in her hands, the rough feel of a ring on her finger digging into my skin.

"Silly, little Rose. I saved you. You're free from that wicked creature now."

"He's not wicked."

"Don't be foolish, Rose. He's a beast."

She pushes me back down and walks off. I lay still as my heart breaks inside me and let the snow cover me in a blanket as cold as the hearts of my fellow villagers.

Sometimes later I hear my mother's voice call out to me. She comes running when she sees me on the ground, I can't imagine how I must look to her; nearly dead from the cold.

I go back to the woods the next day, and the next, and the next, but the border is gone. It has vanished somehow. No matter how frantically I search I can't find it.

And then Mother tells me I am to marry Thomas.

Thomas who had left me for dead in the cold. Thomas who had attacked the only man I ever loved. Thomas with his angry eyes and condescending heart.

Now it's the eve of my wedding. The last night before a miserable life.

I refuse to live it.

But I have no money, no means to escape this town.

Krampus has lived a long time. He told me how he's seen souls leave this world and come back later in a new life.

He is my fate and I am his.

I go to the kitchen and find the biggest knife. Then I don my cloak and head for the woods. I make my way to where the border to his world used to be.

"I'm sorry, meine Liebe," I whisper to the snowy air, hoping against hope that he can hear me somewhere out there.

Then I plunge the knife into my heart.

Part Three: Rose Red & The Beast

Weihnachtszeit

I collapse into Krampus's arms, the aftershock of my orgasm, combined with the flood of memories, racks my body like an earthquake. He holds me close through it. When I'm finally able to get my bearings I prop myself up and look down into his amber eyes. They're so familiar now.

I place my hand against his cheek.

"I know you," I whisper.

He studies me for a moment, and then a smile of true, euphoric joy spreads across his fearsome face. He takes my face in his hands and pulls my mouth down to his.

"Rose," he murmurs against my mouth. "I've been waiting so long."

"I know," I say, kissing him again.

He runs his hands through my hair again.

"I wished for you to stay here until Christmas," he says. "I hadn't planned to tell you about this." He touches the ring again. "The last night I saw you, I wanted to give this to you. To ask you to be mine. I had second-guessed myself for so many nights.

Every time you didn't come to me when you weren't able to escape your village, I told myself how foolish it was to think a beautiful woman like you could love a beast like me."

I slip the ring off my right hand and it to him, placing it gently in his palm.

"Why would you think that?"

"Because I'm a monster."

I hold my left hand out to him. "You very well maybe. The stuff of nightmares and dark myths. You may be absolutely terrible. But I'd rather be an honest monster than a wicked man. Be terrible and love me in all your wicked ways."

He gently takes my left hand and slides the ring onto my ring finger.

"Every day," he says softly, "I have dreamed of you coming back to me."

"And here I am," I say with a smile.

He smiles back. "Here you are."

"Frohe Weihnachten."

He laughs and kisses me again.

"Merry Christmas, meine Schöne."

THE END

Bonus Short Story!

Turn the page for a BONUS short story!

SPIRITS & SPECTERS
A Spring Halloween Tale

Walpurgisnacht

"Would you like to play a game, meine Schöne?"

The voice is like velvet in my ear. I exhale softly, my breath turning to dragon smoke in the winter air.

"Always, mein Herr."

I feel his fanged-smile graze my skin.

"Then *run*."

I do as the beast says and take off through the snowy forest. I only make it a few yards before I hear his heavy breath and the clomping of his hooved-feet across the snow. I hoist my skirts into my hands and run faster. I reach the large oak tree in the center of the forest, halfway to the border, and I press myself up against it.

And then he is there.

He emerges from the shadows of the branches, his chains in one hand and his switch in the other.

"Is that as fast as you can run, meine Schöne?"

"I'm sorry, mein Herr," I pant.

He grins wickedly.

"You were supposed to make it to the border. How can our game be any fun if you end it so soon?"

He steps closer to me and I press back against the tree just a bit more.

"I'm going to have to punish you now for not playing the game correctly."

I bite my lip and remain silent. I don't argue with Krampus when he declares me worthy of punishment. I didn't when I was Rose, and as Monika I ceased doing it after last Krampusnacht.

"What day is it, meine Schöne?"

I shake my head. "Ich weiße nicht," I say.

I don't know.

I see the flicker of amusement in his eyes. He loves when I speak German.

"Is it truly so hard to keep track when you're here? What if you thought it was Sunday and it was really Monday and then you missed a class? A test?" He stands right in front of me, his towering frame looming down over me. "So naughty, meine Schöne. I really must punish you, mustn't I?"

I exhale softly again, I can already feel heat burning in my core.

"Yes, mein Herr."

He drops his switch in the snow and spins me around so that my stomach presses up against the tree trunk. I gasp as the wind is knocked out of me. He begins to wrap his long chains around the tree, binding me to it. He's left my arms free but it doesn't much matter, I can't fight against the weight of the chains.

Once he's done securing me to the oak he comes to stand behind me again. I feel his foot kick between my legs, spreading me wider.

"It's Saturday, meine Schöne. So let's have some fun."

He bunches my dress up in his hand and pulls it up high, exposing my bare bottom to the cold as he tucks the many layers of my dirndl into the chain around my waist. I gasp again as the bitter wind bites at my skin.

"No panties, meine Schöne? How wicked you've chosen to be tonight."

"Es tut mir leid, mein Herr."

He reaches out and wraps his hand around the back of my neck, digging his claws in until I can feel them pierce the skin. "Sorry doesn't matter now, schön Mädchen."

Beautiful girl.

He always speaks so sweetly when he's cruel. I feel a slickness between my thighs at his misleading pet name. He chuckles low, he knows how I love this.

"Ready, meine Schöne?"

"Yes, mein Herr."

He strikes me between my legs with the switch. I wasn't expecting him to start so harshly. I scream from the beautiful pain. He does it again and again with no reprieve. It's been weeks since we've seen each other and he is clearly trying to make up for lost time. By the tenth strike I can tell he plans to pack days worth of pain and punishment into one night. My body quivers at the thought.

"Spread your legs wider," he commands.

I do, the chains digging into my back. I brace my hands against the tree, the bark biting into my skin as Krampus continues to smack my pussy with his switch. Eventually he leaves my red and throbbing cunt alone and moves on to spank the tender flesh between my thighs. He kicks my legs further apart so that I'm practically holding onto the tree to remain upright. With my legs spread and my back arched he has perfect access to the creamy skin between my legs.

He moves the switch back and forth as quickly as he can, causing a never-ending torrent of sharp and hissing pain to shoot through my body.

"Mein Herr," I pant. My safe word dances on the tip of my tongue and I feel the switch halt its onslaught between my legs.

"Monika?" He says softly, the role of punisher vanishing for a moment.

"Keep going," I whisper, resolving myself against the pain. It's horrible but I don't want it to end.

I swear I can *hear* his smile.

He comes up right behind me again and drops to his knees so that his face is at the same level as my sex. He begins to insert his *long* tongue into me and I groan from the delicious invasion. He uses his fangs to nip at me as his tongue delves deep, pressing up against my G-spot. Then he retracts his claws and presses two fingers to my clit and begins to circle it gently.

"Krampus!" I cry out, dying a beautiful death from this sexual torture. "I want to come."

He pulls his tongue out and I whine from the empty feeling left behind.

"You know you're not allowed to come until you scream for me."

I hear him stand up behind me, then he has one hand wrapped around my throat and begins to use the other one to finger me relentlessly.

"Mein Herr," I pant with eyes closed.

"That's it, Monika," he says, "give it all to me."

But I still don't scream. I need more of him. I need to feel every bit of him.

"Please," I whimper.

"Please what?" he hisses in my ear.

"Please fuck me."

"Do you think you deserve that? Have you been punished enough?"

I nod against the tree, all the while we've been speaking he's kept moving his fingers in and out of me.

"Yes?"

He chuckles in my ear then removes his hands from my throat and from in between my legs.

"No!" I cry out from the horrible absence of his touch.

"I won't fuck you until you've been properly punished, meine Schöne, you know this. Now, let's see."

I stiffen in suspense, wondering what he's going to do. Then I hear the sound of his claws popping back out and before I have time to fully process what he plans to do he digs them into my ass and drags down hard, drawing blood and finally causing me to scream.

I hear him chuckle as his tongue makes quick work of lapping up my blood.

"So sweet," he murmurs.

I continue to whimper and moan as he uses his teeth to bite me over and over. By the time this night is done there's no doubt that my ass will be red and bloody and wonderfully marked by my wicked lover.

"Now, Monika," he says, getting back to his feet, "I will fuck you."

"Danke," I gasp.

"Bitte," he growls in my ear as he thrusts his thick cock inside me.

I throw my head back and scream as he pounds into me. His violent ministrations have had me at the peak of coming for so long that it only takes a few moments of his viscous thrusts before I've fallen off the edge and a powerful, euphoric orgasm washes over me.

I know he takes great sexual pleasure in torturing me in this beautiful way, so his release is not long after mine.

When we finish he collapses forward against me, pinning me to the tree and we just breathe heavily in silence for a few minutes. Then he withdraws himself from me and begins to unwrap the chains until I'm free. I turn to face him and smile up at him.

"I love you," I say.

He reaches out and gently wipes some snowflakes from my lashes.

"And I you, Monika. Come," he sweeps me up in his arms, "let's tend to that poor bottom of yours."

It only takes him a few moments to carry me back to his cave and he makes quick work of stripping me out of my clothes and depositing me in the warm bath deep in the cave.

"Aren't you going to join me?" I ask, looking up at where he stands above me.

He smirks. "Not sick of me yet?"

"Never, mein Herr."

He smiles back then takes off his cloak and suede pants and joins me in the water. He pulls me into his lap and begins to gently massage my sore behind. I groan in relaxed pleasure and lean my head against his soft, furry chest.

"It's Walpurgisnacht," he says softly.

"I know," I murmur back.

I almost tell him I know because when Grandma Jo was

alive we celebrated together. We'd have a bonfire on the beach and celebrate together. My Catholic parents found this appalling—their daughter celebrating the ancient pagan festival of Walpurgisnacht. Night of the Witches. Spring Halloween. But I don't dare speak of that woman anymore, especially in front of Krampus. Not since I learned the truth about her last winter.

And while it may be eternally winter here in his realm between the worlds, back in Maryland it's nearly May, spring is in full bloom and my romance with my long lost lover is blossoming as wonderfully as the flowers I planted on the window ledge of my tiny apartment.

"Want to celebrate?" he asks.

I lean back so I can meet his mischievous gaze.

"That depends," I say, "what did you have in mind?"

***

Krampus straightens the flower crown on my head as we stand at the border between the worlds. He steps back and takes in the sight of me. Instead of the plain dirndl I usually wear when I visit his world, he's fashioned me in clothing I left behind in my last life. And it is extravagant. I feel truly magical in my long white dress and emerald green robes.

"You look like a goddess," he says.

"You know the legend around this night?" I ask. "Of Freya and Wotan?"

He smiles down at me. "That they married on the Brocken? Yes, meine Schöne, I know it. And yes, you look like her tonight in all your ethereal, spring glory." I can't help but beam at his words. "I suppose that makes me Wotan? The Devil?"

"You don't even need a costume."

He laughs, shaking his head, then takes my hand in his.

"Very funny," he says as he leads us across the border and into the Harz Mountains of Germany.

It's like stepping into a fairytale. We're in a beautiful, green clearing that is surrounded by various vendor stalls selling everything from jewelry to baked goods. There is a giant bonfire in the center that people are dancing around. They're all dressed in costumes; some in traditional Germanic robes, some like me in Goddess-themed attire, and some are dressed up like witches and devils. I look up at Krampus and gently elbow him in the side.

"See? You don't need a costume."

He smiles then leans down and kisses me. I gasp in surprise against his mouth and he uses that chance to plunge his tongue into mine. I moan softly in pleasure as he digs a hand into my hair, holding my mouth against his. When the kiss finally ends I'm lightheaded.

"Care to dance?" he asks.

"Yes."

We join the revelers around the bonfire and join in the dancing and cheer that surrounds us. No one questions where we came from or how Krampus's 'costume' looks so realistic. I feel nothing but pure joy as I spin around the growing flames with my lover by my side.

As the moon begins to rise higher and higher in the sky Krampus pulls me to the side of the bonfire, out of the way of the other dancers. We walk a little ways off from the clearing and into the surrounding forest.

"What is it?" I ask, somewhat out of breath from all the dancing.

He takes my hands in his and his finger begins to fiddle with the ring on my left hand. The one he gave me many years ago.

"The story of Freya and Wotan…" he says softly, then he drags his eyes up from the ring to meet my gaze. "I love you, Monika. Endlessly. *Eternally*."

"I love you too."

"Then stay with me. Always. Here. Please."

"Here?" I ask, looking around us. "In this forest?"

"Why not?" he says. "There's magic here. I know you feel it too."

He's right. I do.

"I don't want to go back to the snow and the cold and long nights without you. I know you hate school, and all the horrible memories that haunt you back there. I hate the memories that haunt me when you're gone. I'm so tired of spending so much time without you. I want you in my arms forever."

"Krampus," I say, "I'm a mortal."

"You wouldn't be," he says, "if you married me."

I gasp softly.

"Marry me, Monika. Here. Tonight. Under the stars with the spirits and specters as our witnesses the way Freya and Wotan did on the Brocken all those years ago. Pledge to be mine and I will be yours."

"Mein Herr," I whisper. I step forward and press a hand to his cheek. He leans into the touch of my palm and I smile. "My fate was always you."

He leans down and kisses me and this time it's gentle, it's loving, it's a special kind of passion I've never felt with anyone else as long as I've lived. When we break the kiss he leads us deeper into the forest until we reach a small clearing where the moonlight shines bright. We stand in the middle and hold hands.

I've been wearing his ring on my left ring finger for months, but it was always just a promise. This—*this* is an act. We will bind our souls together so that they can never be severed again.

The woods around us begin to rumble with ancient magic as vines and moss begin to creep up our legs and down our arms, wrapping around us like ribbons. A beautiful binding ritual made up of forest floor findings and powerful magic.

"I vow," he begins, "to always love you. To protect you. To care for you. To be your champion. I—" he gets choked up and I realize that there are tears in his eyes.

"I vow," I say softly, "to always come home to you."

"Monika, you *are* my home."

"And you are mine."

The vines and moss bindings tug against us, pushing us closer together. I instinctively rest my head against his chest so that I can hear his heartbeat. The steady rhythm is comforting.

"Forever," he whispers.

"Forever," I whisper back.

THE END

Thank You!

Thank you so much for reading this spicy holiday tale! If you enjoyed this story and would be willing to leave a review on Amazon and/or Goodreads it would be the world to me! Reviews are a great way to support authors.

You can also support my writing by donating to my patreon! patreon.com/magicalmolly
Patrons get exclusive content including, bonus short stories, behind the scenes sneak peeks of upcoming projects, extra artwork, etsy store discounts, and acknowledgments in all my books!

Which brings me to a **VERY SPECIAL THANK YOU** to my patrons:
Bianca DK
Haley Hardaway
Josie
Mallory Kjar
Katy L.
Sarah Leppert

Thank You!

Sarah (smcc)
John Smith

CHECK OUT SOME OF MY OTHER TITLES
Riding The Headless Horseman (The Legends of Arletta
Harrington Book 1)
Loved Alone: An Edgar Allan Poe Gothic Horror
Falling for Jack Frost: A Dark Fantasy Holiday Romance
Be Terrible: A Holiday Monster Romance
Not a Myth (co-authored by Marcia Ruiz-Olguín)
The Willow's Silence (co-authored by Marcia Ruiz-Olguín)
The Fable of Wonderland (co-authored by Marcia
Ruiz-Olguín)

*All books available in paperback & FREE on Kindle Unlimited! Get
signed copies on my*
https://www.etsy.com/shop/authormollylikovich

Acknowledgments

Thank you to the folks who made this new special edition possible! Thank you to my assistant, editor, and cover artist River Meade. You are always a delight to collaborate with creatively and I am forever grateful for how you bring the images in my mind to life. Thank you to the beta readers and arc readers from 2021 and everyone who has since read the book and posted a review and shared it around. Thank you to my patrons and everyone in the Magical Molly discord server. Thank you my mother for always believing in these projects. Thank you to Lady Marcia, obviously. And thank you to Wendy.

About the Author

Molly Likovich is the Amazon Bestselling Author of *Riding The Headless Horseman.* She is also the author of *Loved Alone* and *Falling for Jack Frost.* She is the co-author of *Not a Myth, The Willow's Silence,* and *The Fable of Wonderland* with her best friend and creative partner Marcia Ruiz-Olguín. She has a BA in Creative Writing from Salisbury University, her poetry and short stories have appeared in numerous literary magazines and journals, and in 2020 she was a finalist in the L. Ron Hubbard Writers of the Future Contest. When she's not writing, she's working as an actor and playwright for A Cow Jumped Over The Moon Theater. She currently resides in her hometown in Maryland with her dachshund, Prancer.

To learn more visit www.mollylikovich.com

Follow Molly online: Instagram, Twitter, & TikTok
@magicalmolly

Made in United States
Troutdale, OR
10/27/2024